Out to Lunch

Peggy Perry Anderson

Green Light Readers
HOUGHTON MIFFLIN HARCOURT
BOSTON NEW YORK

To Jack, Jorie, Jeffery and Jinger,
our nieces and nephews
who prepared us for parenthood.

The Library of Congress cataloged the hardcover edition as follows:
Out to lunch/by Peggy Anderson
p. cm.
Summary: A mischievous frog makes a scene when his parents take him out to a fancy restaurant to eat.
[Restaurants—Fiction. 2. Behavior—Fiction. 3. Frogs—Fiction. 4. Stories in rhyme.]
Title.
PZ8.3.A54840u

ISBN: 978-0-544-52858-1 paperback
ISBN: 978-0-544-56819-8 paper over board

Manufactured in China
SCP 10 9 8 7 6 5 4 3 2 1

4500535519

"Out to eat.
What a treat!"

1

"Too bad," Joe's mother said,
"our babysitter was sick in bed."

"We're ready to eat.
Just give us a seat!"

"Do you have crayons or playgrounds?" asked Joe.

The waiter said no.

"Mind your manners well today.
We're out to lunch, not out to play."

"I'll have pie and cake.
NO PEAS!"

Mother said,
"One child's meal, please."

"I'm a reindeer!" said Joe.

"Now where did he go?"

"Peek-a-boo! I see you."

"Remember what I said today.
We're out to lunch, not out to play."

"Yippee! Yippee! Food for me!"

Joe slurped.

Joe burped.

"Uh-oh," said Joe.

"There's an itch on my toe."

"The table is no place for feet.
Please, Joe, sit still and eat."

Joe dropped his fork.

Joe dropped his spoon.

Joe launched his fish stick to the moon.

"JOE, SIT STILL!"

"Oh, dear. There's a fly in here!"

"Don't worry. I'll get him, Dad!"

WHAP!

ZAP!

"Best fly I ever had!"

"Okay, Joe, it's time to go."

"Out to eat. What a treat!"